CERA HANO

Vwriynn

The Tale Of Flame And Shadow: Part III

To my king.

Contents

Foreword

Contents

Acknowledgement

Michael Runk

Reiki Master/Teacher Intuitive Tarot Advisor

Michael completed his initial Reiki training in 2004 and his Master training in 2005. In early February 2020, he completed his advanced Holy Fire III Karuna Reiki Master training. As with his Reiki journey, his journey with the cards began in 2004, and they have been a part of his life ever since. Michael has been reading professionally since early 2020, having read for clients worldwide. He now provides a full range of Reiki services and Tarot readings and teaches students who wish to learn either or both disciplines.

Stay In Touch

Michael can be reached at Reikibymike@gmail.com Follow him at: Facebook: Reiki by Mike or Six of Cups Tarot Twitter: @reikibymike TikTok: @six_of_cups_tarot Instagram: Reiki by Mike/Six of Cups Tarot

David Bailey

Rune Master

I have been a paranormal investigator for nearly 13 years. I've read Tarot for almost a year and Runes for about six months. I am a Twitch streamer under the name DramaTroll.

Stay In Touch

TikTok: Divination David Website: www.paranormalhive.live

SERENA

The journey through the portal would've never prepared me for what greeted us on the other side. A gentle road that leads to a posted sign labeled 'Wethidarin Village' is somewhat discernible despite the many cracks and holes given to it by the elements.

Gardens are bustling with insect life who've made their home in the tall grasses and overgrown bushes.

Some doors look collapsed or were perhaps destroyed by looters or animals as time passed. Either way, they left a welcoming entrance for anyone needing shelter. There were signs of fires; in some cases, it was merely a trail of soot and smoke above a windowpane; in others, it was a pile of ash where once a building stood.

"Where are we?" I asked while continuing to look at this ghost town. There seems only to be wildlife and no sign of people.

"We are in Vwirynn," Davi answers, and I look at him. The book is still clutched firmly in his grip as his bag of runes sits tied to his hip.

"Did you get the coordinates wrong?" Alwin asks.

"No. The runes never lie. This realm is called Vwirynn, or, as the description in the Grimoire read, shadowlands. It looks pretty bleak and shadowy to me." Davi answers him. The temperature is cool but not freezing like Whitfrost. Our thick cloaks are unnecessary in this environment.

I move towards them and allow my wings to flex. "We should shed our thick clothing. I don't think we will need it here."

They both nod, and I glamour my wings while shedding my thick wool coat and tunic. "I was wearing a short black shirt, strapped in, and tan pants and boots." Odith's tarot deck is tucked inside my cargo pants pocket. I found it back in Xora, thinking she left it there before she killed me the second time. I'm not a master, but something inside me called to them as they called me.

"Is there a map in that book?" I ask Davi, pointing at it. He flips it open only in his black short-sleeved crimson tunic, pants, and boots. He thumbs a page before looking at me.

"Here. This realm is vast. I'm unsure where we will locate this king and shadow master." Davi admits. I took the book from him and looked at the map. The cartography is beautiful, capturing the different elements of each city and village of this world. To include routes directing us. I could fly, but I haven't had much practice.

Then I would leave these two alone; I know Alwin might kill Davi if I do that. Despite my anger towards the Rune Master for what he did to Niya, we need him.

"We need to find civilization. But I do not see any place close to us that might have a semblance of a community." I let out a sigh. "Looks like we are in for a long walk. According to the map, we will need to travel south down this path until reaching a fork in the road and turn southeast along that small mountain range." But I will welcome this time needed for Alwin and me. It will give us more time to connect on an emotional level rather than an intimate one.

An hour or so passed, and we'd only made a few short remarks here and there about this world we're now in. It's awkward, and I know it shouldn't be. "Alwin, is something bothering you?"

He gives me a side eye before answering as the small rocks knock against our boots. "Just thinking of our mission. Of where everyone from home went during the fight with Odith. Master Mikao stayed there with a few to help rebuild it, but it still bothers me, knowing I won't be there to help. It will be new when this is all over with saving the Confessor and Rose and going to war with Queen Lilac. And perhaps–" He sighs.

"They won't need you anymore?" I finished for him. He nods. "I don't think that's true. Master Mikao, although I don't know him as well as you do, doesn't seem like the kind to keep you at arm's length. He'll need your help to replace the teachers that were killed."

"Perhaps you'll join me."

"I'm no teacher. I can barely control what power I have. How do you expect me to teach others how to control theirs? To master their weapons. Pekka was the master of combat." An invisible punch to both our guts at the memory of him.

Alwin stops briefly; we watch as Davi takes the lead further down the path. "When this is all over, we'll both be needed to guide the future generations in the new world. Half-elves will never go away, nor will humans who intend on our persecution." I drop my head, understanding what he means. His thumb and forefinger grip my chin, lifting it to meet his gaze. "Whatever we face, no matter what, we do it together. That's what these mean."

He places our hands over each other's hearts where our mate emblem is imprinted into our skin. A reminder of who we are to one another and the great lengths we will go through to be together, including death.

"Alwin and Serena, you both should come look at this." Davi's voice cuts through our bubble, and Alwin smirks at me before placing a chaste kiss on my lips.

"Let's go see what Puny wants. It's probably nothing but a dead snake." We make our way to the Rune Master, and what I see is much larger than a tiny reptile. "As you were saying?" I looked over at my mate, who didn't seem amused.

"What happened to him?" Davi asked as I bent down to examine the corpse of a young boy who hadn't reached adolescence yet by the baby fat still lining his cheeks. His body is gray and laced with black veins popping out his arms, neck, and shins. Two black holes remain where his eyes used to be. I raise my hand to touch him, but Alwin snatches my wrist in warning.

"We don't know what killed him. It could be a contagious illness." he explains, and I nod.

"It was no ailment that took him." We spin on our heels, the three of us withdrawing weapons, ready for the stranger neither of us heard approaching. The voice belonged to an older woman, around her seventieth year of life, judging by the white hair and gray clouds mixing with what used to be bright blue eyes. A cane helps her walk towards us, the rags draped around her, leaving a drag mark in the soft dirt.

"Do you know this boy?" I asked, stepping between the men and her. My fire returns inside while I wait for the others to follow my lead. She doesn't appear to be a threat, but the caution has been there since my time in the in-between.

The older woman slowly kneels next to him, placing a hand on his forehead and the other over his heart. I watch her eyes close, and she hums a tune before swiping her hand over his lids to make it look like he is sleeping. "This shadow magic. The boy was a part of the punishment the villagers back in Wethidarin received for defying the King."

I help her to her feet, ensuring she's well-balanced before creating some space between us once more. "Who is the King?"

"He goes by many names, but most know him as Alistair." Alwin meets my eye at the name.

"Do you know where we can find him?" Davi asks before I get the chance to. The older woman laughs and then notices how serious we

4

all are.

"No one finds the Shadow King. He rules from the blind spots of the naked eye. Using his magic to conquer and kill those that would defy him." She grunts and then begins walking further ahead, leaving us with the corpse. "If you want to find him, just go to where all the souls of Vwirynn end up."

I ran beside her, not wanting her to leave without further explanation. "Where is that, exactly?" She raises a brow at me but continues her forward progress. "We're not from here. I wish to speak with him. I have vitae information for him."

That catches her attention.

She turns to look at me, assessing me from head to foot before gesturing for me to bend to meet her eye.

"What are you?" Her hand presses against my forehead before I get a chance to answer, but she screams and jerks her hand away. The sound of sizzling skin and the smell of burnt flesh made my eyes water. When I look at her, those eyes are widened, and the humor from before is quickly replaced with terror.

I reach out to offer to heal her, but she flinches, and a firm hand grips my shoulder, pulling me back against a complex form. "We need to go, Serena. There's nothing you can do for her."

Alwin interlocks his fingers into mine, pulling me down the path until we sprint. We don't stop until we're a far enough distance away that Alwin doesn't fear for our safety. I raise my hands above my head, catching my breath as Alwin gets our water out. Taking a refreshing gulp, I look back behind us. I know she wouldn't be able to see us, but it frightens me knowing what I did to her.

"I burned her without calling my power." It escapes in a whisper, my words laced with confusion.

"You're a Phoenix, Serena; your fire is constant," Alwin explains. "I could've killed her. She still might die from an infection

5

because of burning her." I face away from him, close my eyes, and think of things that would cool me down being back in Whitfrost surrounded by snow and ice.

"You're not a monster, Serena." Alwin's in front of me. His scent washing over me had the calming effect I needed. His firm hands are on my cheeks, and he kisses me softly. "You don't burn me.

Clearly, your essence deemed her as a threat, and it defended you. My shadows have done the same for me. I've just had a much longer learning how to sense it."

"Will I ever learn to control it?"

"Open your eyes." he whispers, and I hesitate but listen. "You have more control than you think you do." I follow his gaze to the ground but then grip his arms as I notice they float in the air. My wings gently flapped behind us. "Whatever you feel comes to life. You wanted to escape, but not without me, so your wings answered the call. Use your emotions to communicate with your essence, Serena, and you'll be in command."

I think about landing, and slowly, we return to solid ground.

My wings dissipate once more, and I embrace my mate with gratitude. Davi clears his throat, reminding us of his presence, and we walk apart to approach him. He had the map out and began to tell us where we were.

"While you two were up there, I was deciphering what the old woman said. You see, we're here." He points to the backside of a mountain ridge. "Which, as you can see, is just beyond the horizon." We follow his pointer finger and see the pointed outline. "Now, there is something about her mentioning souls of this world and where they all end up. Just east of Nightingale City is the Sea of Souls. In the farthest southeast is an island with no name. I think that's where we're meant to go."

"Can you portal us there?" I ask.

6

He digs into his bag of runes and nods. "I can, but there's a small catch."

"What?" Alwin growls.

"I might not have enough power to bring us back to Whitfrost." We look at him, waiting for him to elaborate. "Runes are not just carved pieces of stone that automatically come with power. They're created. It takes certain ingredients and materials to make more. I siphon the magic from each piece I use, and once it's served its purpose, the stone turns blank and becomes useless."

"What do you need?" Alwin asks.

Davi shuffles in his bag, pulls out a parchment, and begins to read, "I'll need to borrow some essence from one of you. I prefer Serena since she's the more powerful one." Alwin snarls. "No offense, Dark One, but as you keep reminding her, she's the first true Phoenix in two centuries."

"You're not taking an ounce of my mate's power. Find another way."

"There is none. Unless you find another Rune Master running around the universe, then by all means."

I step between them, defusing the situation before it escalates further. "Davi can use my essence if we can get around quicker.

Remember, Niya and Rose don't have much time on their side. I'd hate to think what would happen to them because you're too possessive to let me lend a little magic." I narrow my eyes at Alwin, who scoffs but nods. "What else do you need for the spell?"

"Bones from a dragon. Wouldn't you happen to know any of those, would you?" Davi inquires, his gaze looking past me.

"Braxor wouldn't defile his death to help you."

"No, but he might if you asked him," I said, and Alwin went quiet. Running his fingers through his long white hair. "When the time is right, we must call him."

"There's no guarantee he'll answer from this realm," Alwin explains. "But I will attempt because it's what you want. And it's what we need to help Rose and the Confessor."

"Good, then let's get started," Davi states, pulling out his relics and reciting the magic needed to port us to another part of this realm. I grip Alwin's hand, neither knowing what danger awaits us on the other side nor knowing we're together.

"In this life and the next." he whispers. "Always."

ALWIN

The smell is the first thing I notice, aside from the mud slick against our boots and coated against our skin.

"You couldn't have aimed us away from the mud pool?" I snarled.

"Portals are unpredictable, Dark One; you, of all people, should know that by now." Davi wipes his hands down his shirt and then looks ahead. I do the same searching for Serena. When I don't see her, my heart rate begins to rise as the last time I couldn't find her, she was drying.

"Serena?" I scan the area, first the skies, to see if she took flight, then the ground for any sign she walked away. "Where is she?"

Davi searches the distance, but there's nothing to see but large, sharpened rocks and the slosh we've landed in. "Serena!" he calls out.

Our voices echo off the open space while we trudge through the mud. The humidity here is stifling. Sweat coats my forehead after five minutes, and I'm wiping it from my eyes. Every inhale I take is covered with a thick earthly flavor, causing my throat and mouth to dry out quickly. Grabbing my water from my bag, I open it to drink from only a drop that hits my tongue. Confused, I squeeze the leather pouch, but there's nothing left.

"Mine's empty, too," Davi says breathlessly. "They were nearly full when we left."

9

"It's got to be the environment here. Evaporated our water from our pouches just as quickly as it appears to be doing from our bodies."

He's right. I can feel the dehydration kicking in and look ahead for shelter from the sun. "We need to get out of this sun's path.

Serena will find us."

"Where do you suggest we go?" Davi asks. I point to the mountain range just ahead. "Right."

The journey was arduous, navigating through the dense ground before it transitioned into solid rock. When shielded from the sun's rays, our bodies pressed against the exceptionally smooth stone, both of us running low on energy. "Without water, we won't survive this heat," Davi states. He's right; although he has magic, he's still human. I may come back from the brink of death, but not Puny. "The map shows a stream at the end of this valley. A sort of oasis by the looks of the trees. We make it there, hydrate, and then follow up to look for her."

The turmoil I feel for leaving where we landed without her has my insides twisting. That and the lack of water. Davi and I use the last of what we have to walk the shadows of the valley, keeping contact with the stone as it seems to be keeping us more relaxed. My ears twitch at the sound of water flowing, and I perk up the second I see it.

We drop our sacks together and race to the bank, dipping our hands into the surprisingly cold liquid. I cup my hands together and bring a small puddle to my lips, their dryness longing to taste its refreshing texture.

"Stop!" Serena's scream catches my attention, and she's next to me. She knocked the water from my hands, wiped them clean, and looked at me with fear. "Did you drink it?" I don't answer her immediately; I try to ensure she isn't an illusion. "Alwin, did you drink the water?"

I shake my head from side to side and gently caress her cheek. She pulls out her waterskin, pops the cork off, and holds it to my lips. The fresh, crisp liquid easily floods my throat, and I want more, but she pulls it away. "Not too much. We need to conserve what we have. Davi, you need some, too."

She reaches in his direction without looking, her focus mainly on me. I follow her arm and see the Rune Master violently shaking on the ground. Without my full strength, I can barely move. "Serena." My voice is scratchy.

"Don't speak. You'll need to be healed. Davi," she looks over and finally realizes why he hasn't answered her. Racing to him, she rolls him on his side. "You drank it, didn't you? Idiot." She scolds him while supporting his head until he finally stops moving. Using a cloth from her belt, she wipes his mouth before turning on his back and listening to his heart. "It's faint. We must return him to Master Mikao now, or he'll die."

"How?" My voice croaks, and I crawl over to them, hating my weakness.

"I don't know, Alwin, but without his runes and no Tarot Master, we're stuck here. Maybe you should call Braxor. Can't dragons fly across worlds?" Her tongue is sharp, and she's concerned about the Rune Master. Whether that be because Serena has a pure heart or our best chance at saving the Confessor, Rose is currently cradled in her arms.

"No. But I can try some Rieke."

"You know how?"

I've been watching Master Mikao for many years. I was learning his techniques and ways of using the essence to heal the sick and wounded. Looking down at Puny, I inhale sharply and let it go before taking more water from her just for the extra boost. I place one hand on his forehead and the other on his heart. "Serena, I'll need your help to heal him. If I use too much of my life force, I may not survive this."

"How does this work?" she asks. I place her hands in the same spots mine were, then touch her hands with my mind. Our skin buzzes to life with our essence.

"I want you to close your eyes and focus on your soul. Reiki works to create a state of equilibrium in our life-force energy. When you feel his soul reaching out to you, don't block it."

"How will I know?"

"Because I'll be there with you. Now, close your eyes and find your peace." I do the same, thinking of the ways Master Mikao would instruct others to clear their minds of everything and focus on the one thing or image that's always brought them peace. I searched my memories and found one of when I was a child, eating gooseberry pie fresh from the oven. It was my favorite. The bursting flavor brings a smile to my face.

I exhale on three counts and then repeat while inhaling. Davi's aura quickly finds me, and I reach out to him. Runes paint his pale skin, and his eyes are sunken in. He looks smaller than usual, and I see creatures of bones sticking prongs inside him. "Serena, where are you?"

She doesn't answer, and I'm no longer inside my body. Everything that is happening is going on inside of the Rune Master. I charge forward, trying to pull them from him, but they're stuck like a moth to the flame. "Dark One."

Davi's soul pleads for help as a shaky hand, nearly nothing but bone reaches for me. When I feel the last of him pulling away, a blast of fire knocks into a creature and appears, not in her regular form, but as a Phoenix, my mate. She blasts the other three from Davi's body and quickly lands. Her nails gently grasped my outstretched fingers.

I place Davi's hands over mine and Serena's chest while putting mine against his. "Let it flow, Serena. Give him some of your life force, or we'll lose him for good."

She makes a bird-like noise, which I assume means she understands, and in a few more seconds, I watch as my shadow and her flames dance along his skin like vines on a tree. The essence we've freed up, sinking into him, rejuvenating his soul again. I break the connection before he takes too much and is knocked backward.

I blinked the brain fog away and sat up, looking at Serena sit- ting beside him, appearing unaffected by what we just did. When I go back to them, I see the color come back to the Rune Master's face, his eyes no longer shrouded in darkness, and the pink tinge a human has surfacing back in his lips.

"Serena, are you okay?" She smiles at me.

"I am. I believe you just performed your first healing session, Rieke Apprentice." she said, pride glowing in her eyes.

"We don't know if it worked. Or how well it did. Plus, we used part of our essence to do it. I don't know what the consequences of magic like this could mean." I warned her.

"Guys?" Davi wakes, and Serena helps him sit up. "Don't drink the water."

"Yeah. I figured the name Sea of Souls would be enough warning." Serena deadpans. "Either way, the sun appears to be setting soon. We'll camp here tonight and plot our next move tomorrow."

"One problem with that," I say, and they look at me for further explanation. "Water. Your one water skin won't be enough for the three of us. We have dried meat left for food, but I imagine that is scarce here, too. It would be best to travel at night while the sun isn't beating down on us."

"Davi will need to rest, and so will you." Serena persisted. "No. I will carry him. I'm already feeling better, Serena. Trust

me." She looks at me and then at the Rune Master before nodding in agreement.

"Then so be it. We only travel at night."

After getting Davi back on his feet, with both of us supporting his weight, we decided to head back in the direction we came. The island appears to be much larger than we anticipated. The Oasis of Trees is on the other side of the mountains and doesn't show us needing to cross a stream of soul creatures. That's what Serena is calling them, to reach it. We decided that climbing would take longer and more energy than we had to spare.

Ten minutes into our hike, Davi lets Serena walk ahead as he limps while baring his weight against me. It's awkward, and I bite my tongue with the many unkind things I could say to him because I know by the look in his eyes.

"Thank you, Dark One. For saving me." I roll my eyes.

"If Serena didn't ask me to, you'd be soul creature food, and I wouldn't shed a single tear for you. After all, what fate does an adulterous traitor have bestowed upon him?" It appears I can't hold my tongue when it comes to him.

"Whatever the gods decide, I'm sure it will be what I deserve." He answers in a humble tone that rubs me the wrong way.

"Who will take your place?" I inquire, genuinely curious, as there can only be one Rune Master at a time. He can name an apprentice, but the essence and relics don't pass on until he does.

"Trying to figure out how much longer I can be useful to you and your Phoenix?" he asks, but I don't entertain his question. A sigh escapes him as he answers, "There are a few ways to know when my apprentice is nearby or how to find them. One uses the runes themselves to locate their next master. But the other, well, it's much more. They have to be immune to all magic except for the Amazons. I didn't know that one until my first encounter with the Queen. But your shadow magic and Confessor powers."

"I see. So how did you get chosen?"

"The runes found me." he says. "When I was a boy, I ventured into a cave just beyond a waterfall while playing a game with my little sister. In the pool were shimmering white tiles that made me think of pearls. We weren't wealthy, so I figured they could benefit me. I was taken into another realm when I swam to the bottom and touched them. A world

14

between worlds where only Rune Master's past, present, and future can venture. That was where I learned everything. When I was sent back, the life I once knew wasn't there anymore. The realm was overrun with pure blood, and I was a man. It felt like hours in the in-between, but on the outside, it was years

—something to do with time not existing.

"I went to find my family and discovered the village I grew up in was empty. Not a single livestock insight. That's when I used the runes for the first time. Portal me to where my family is." He stops for a moment, the pain of his past coming to life in his eyes, and I find sympathy for him for a moment.

"What happened?" My voice is softer than usual.

He turns to look at me. "They were dead. Their bodies were tossed into fire pits amongst thousands of others. I swore on them that day I'd get revenge on who did this to them. To our home."

"Did you ever find out?"

He nods. "Queen Lilac's father ordered the slaughter of my home so he could conquer that realm. They even built a palace and battalion there. I haven't been back since."

"What realm? I know you are not from Xora or Whitfrost."

Davi unhooks his arm from my shoulders and pulls his shirt off to reveal his inked torso. "Right between the shoulders. I got it tattooed days after I saw what happened." I read the word in my head over and over, knowing I'd never been there or heard of it until now. "Ulorea. The place where nothing but humans thrived until the former King of Xora marched across our lands and destroyed it."

"Is that how you ended up in service to his daughter?" He covers himself back up and looks on ahead. Serena's bright flame kept her in our line of sight.

"Yes. Let's call it a failed assassination attempt. Lilac has magic. I'm unsure how it happened, but I hope to find out one day. Right before I gut her."

"Alwin and Davi, have you two passed out again?" Serena calls us, and we no longer speak about Davi's past. When we catch up to her, she's looking at the map, her small ball of fire illuminating it from the side. She moves her hand behind it, careful to keep it from catching. "Do you see that?"

"Unbelievable," Davi whispers.

"At least we're heading in the right direction." she says. Her little flame has revealed hidden ink showing the location of the one city on the godforsaken island. "Alistair's palace must be in the middle of the oasis. If we pick up the pace, we'll make it to the edge by morning."

"I'll carry, Puny." I don't wait for an object as I lift him across my shoulders and lead the way.

"A little warning would've been nice." He grunts, my shoulder digging into his gut.

"That's where you have me wrong, Puny. I'm not nice." "You're nice to Serena."

"She's my mate and the one who warms my bed at night. My future wife and mother of my children."

"Good point, Dark One."

16

SERENA

Alwin and Davi continue to banter back and forth about senseless things. Meanwhile, I'm focusing on guiding us through a world none have ever been to while maintaining my fire.

The heat here didn't bother me. Something about my essence is protecting me, and I have no desire to drink as often as those two.

I don't mind knowing I can provide them with the necessary resources to survive in this place. As we approach the beginning of the tree line, I signal for us to stop. We don't know what potential dangers are lurking within those trees, and I don't have enough energy to go through another Rieke session.

Alwin and Davi catch up to me, silent aside from the shallow breaths they're taking. My mate shows strength even when carrying his bag and another person's body weight. I look towards the sky, trying to judge when the sun will rise, but nothing gives its position away. "We don't know what lurks in the shadows. I don't want to put us at risk."

Alwin gently sets Davi back on the ground, narrowing his eyes as I see him summon his shadow magic. His eyes go entirely black while the hum of essence vibrates from his body into mine. Our emblem comes to life on my chest as it recognizes its match. "There's nothing aside from a waterfall in the middle of the oasis. Any sign of life can't

17

be for a mile as far as I can see."

"So we keep going?" Davi asks more than states.

I look at my mate, whose eyes fade to standard color, and he nods. "We keep going until we can't. Drink up. The fates might bless us with clean water once inside the shade of the trees."

Moving ahead, Davi walks alone, benefiting from the additional rest, and he enjoys full access to the water. Alwin made the same choice as me. At this moment, the Rune Master is more useful when alive than when dead. Since neither of us can port back home, Braxor has not come since Alwin called an hour ago. He believes the dragon will see if and when we truly need him.

I cautiously step over the wood line, keeping my flame ahead of us, and see an artificial path of stones leading further into the small forest. We kept as quiet as possible, moving at a pace Davi could tolerate. It doesn't take long for the water flow to catch my ears. I lead us to the sound; the desire to taste fresh water makes my mouth water. I've not gone this long without a drink since I was a girl. Days in Narborim weren't so kind to my mother and me. I am being fatherless, living in a rotting home with little to no food and scarce water rationed by the village elders.

The day the Gnaxtor came was a blessing and curse. Being taken in by Niya's family helped me stay alive, but it also meant never seeing my mother again. Those days have long since passed, and I have a new purpose. A new family that found me, and I intend to bring it back together before the end of this war.

Through the thick foliage, I see a shimmering blue glow coming from behind it. I push through, the sharpened thorns of vines pricking at my skin, but I don't care because I can smell the deca-dent taste of water. Pressing on, I bring my essence to help protect my skin, burning whatever touches it and race to the pool's edge. It's beautiful, clear, and soulless.

"Serena, are you sure it's safe?" Alwin asks from my right side. I cup my hands, dip them into the liquid, bring them to my lips, and sip. The fresh, crisp, cool water soothes my dry throat as I slowly swallow. I lock eyes with my mate as he watches me. I'm waiting to see if I'll react Davi did to the other stream. Nothing feels off, and I take another handful and bring it to Alwin's lips. After he tries it, we wait another moment before grabbing and filling the empty water skin.

I look to tell Davi, but he's dunked his head into it. A laugh bubbles in my chest at the sight of him. "Be careful, Rune Master, you might drown."

He surfaces, his hair sticking to his forehead, mouth dripping wet. "It tastes better than death."

"Doesn't everything?" I ask.

"Right." Davi fills the water skin he is holding and caps it.

After we all seemed filled to the brim with as much water as we could handle without dying, we were back on our feet again. "Should we rest here for the night?"

"Yes. Puny will need to rest and eat." Alwin replies.

"Davi set up for the night. I'll go get some firewood." I place my bag down next to Alwin's and get moving. Lighting the end of a fallen branch with my flame as I pile other dry ones. Next are fallen leaves for the kindling. I've been using my essence for hours, my power running dangerously low, and my stomach twists with hunger.

A nearby branch cracks, causing me to freeze. Scanning the area, I finally spot it—the creature with bramble-colored fur, almost melding into the night. However, nothing eludes my light. Crouching down, I empty my hands and approach slowly. With a flick of my fingers, I direct a fireball straight at its exposed side, relishing the satisfying sound upon impact. "Good shot." I cringe at the sound of Alwin's voice. "Didn't hear you coming."

He follows me to the game. "That's because darkness and I are like twin flames. I have control overshadows and everything to do with it. Using them to keep me hidden is one of the first skills I mastered as a boy."

"Tell me more." He takes a seat next to me in the soft grass. "About your life growing up. You know about mine."

He ran a hand through his long hair, whether from nerves or to get it out of his eyes; I couldn't tell. "There's not much to it. My father trained me since the second I could summon my first glimpse of shadow. Every day, it was the same: learning the history of our race, exercising for hours, and when I wasn't physically more assertive, he'd try to strengthen my mind by using different tactics to test my mental barriers. One of the worst visions, probably his favorite to use, was of my future wife dying and me not being there to protect her.

"A glimpse into my future if I failed my lessons. After weeks of feeling that loss tore me apart, I built a solid wall. When he got through torturing me with her, he moved on to my children. They would be more powerless, dragged off by humans to use as leverage against the next Shadow King. What I saw, it's something I wouldn't wish on any parent. Then, and I'm sure he regrets this one, it was my mother. He knew how close our bond was, and for a little while, I thought he envied our bond.

"He would have her beheaded for giving birth to me. That was her crime, and unfortunately, her death became a reality even though he couldn't stop." Tears swelled in his eyes, and I interlaced my fingers with him, providing him with comfort. "I guess that was the real test. When it came down to it, neither of us could protect the person we loved most."

"Alwin, you can't blame yourself."

"But I do." He snaps, then he sighs. "I'm sorry. It's hard for me to imagine her ever since the cave in the Fenix Mountains."

"She sacrificed her soul for me, and that's something I'll never be able to repay her, but I'm eternally grateful because it brought me back to you. To Niya, Rose, and even Davi." I smiled.

"Puny seems to be growing on you." he comments.

"Despite all the bad, there is good in him. I believe he can be redeemed."

"Second chance?" He quirked a brow.

"Everyone deserves one. He didn't kill Niya. Not saying that what he did was excusable because it wasn't." I sigh, cup Alwin's cheek, and look deep into his before saying this next part. I hope he understands it's more for him than the Rune Master. "No matter our mistakes, big or small, they all mean one thing... that we still have a soul. Davi is human; they tend to make many mistakes, but having lived with humans all my life, I've realized that's how they learn, how we all learn. The only difference is, we don't let it define or defeat us."

He leans forward, pressing his forehead to mine. "You have a way with words, Serena."

His lips meet mine. Our kiss is initially soft but grows more intense as our desire to mate surfaces. Alwin's hand landed on my hips, lifting me to straddle him. A growl of hunger interrupts the beginnings of what I can only assume would be a heated session of sex against a tree. "We need to eat."

"I'm hungry for you, Phoenix."

"Ah, but the rabbit will give me the fuel to keep you up the rest of the night." I wink and move to get off him, but his fingers dig into my sides, and he pushes me down on his ready cock.

"How long will you tease me?"

"We're on a mission, and as much as I'd love to strip you down and make love to you in that pool of water, we're pressed for time. Besides, we must wash and have enough energy to face whatever fate will test us when the sun comes up."

He whimpers, pleading in his eyes, but lets me go.

Back at the camp, I get the fire going while Alwin tends to the rabbit. I was skinning it and getting it cleaned for us to roast it. There isn't much to the meat, but enough for us to enjoy along with the leftover portions we brought.

"I'll take the first watch," I state, and Alwin nods. The one thing I've always admired about him is that he doesn't try to control me. And most certainly doesn't treat me like a damsel in distress. He respects my need to contribute to the team.

The noise from the water. I have to stand so I do not fall asleep.

It drowns out the snores coming from Davi, which is a bonus. There is no gap in the canopy of trees, which prevents me from gazing at the stars. With nothing else to occupy my time, I pull out the tarot deck that's been burning a hole in my pocket since I placed it back there a few days ago.

I try to remember watching Niya's technique as she shuffled them. I know she usually pulled three cards for herself and then interpreted them. Growing up with her, she taught me the meaning of the cards or potential interpretations of them. Their feel is smooth, but there's a heaviness to them. One wouldn't think parchment could weigh this much, but when the fates play apart–

"Show me something," I whisper and pull the first card. Staring back at me is the *Temperance*. An image of a woman in robes with angel wings pouring equal parts liquid into two vases is painted on it. I rack my brain trying to remember what Niya said this could mean. Next, I draw *The Emperor* and then *The High Priestess*. Both honorable and regal cards by the looks of the figures painted to sit on thrones. All three cards sit placed on my lap as I study them.

This reminds me of when Niya gave me my first reading just one month after I got to the church.

We were sitting on the rug in her room; she was dressed in white robes, shuffling her deck. I was wearing pants and a shirt gifted to me by the family.

22

"Are you ready?" she asks. "Go for it," I replied.

She lays out three cards, all painted with funny little images. One at a time, she explained them to me.

"Temperance could mean inspiration or protector. You could be destined for a greater purpose." Greater purpose, how could she mean that for a poor half-elf orphan girl? *"This next one,"* she pointed at the one with the painted lady on it, *"the High Priestess means you have a sense of mystery about you. Or in need of enlightenment. But don't be afraid because The Emperor has many meanings, too. One could be leadership.*

Maybe you'll become some Illuminate."

I sighed. I'm unsure why this raven-haired girl wanted to play nice with me or give me false hope for *a brighter future.*

"That's it. These cards again." My voice is louder than I meant for it to be, and Davi stirs while Alwin pops a brow at me. "Go back to sleep."

He sits up, placing his elbows on his knees before speaking, "I can't sleep knowing we'll be heading into unknown territory and tomorrow to tell a man that we were originally sent here to assassinate him." I gesture for him to come to me, and he does. "Playing with cards like the Confessor?"

"Not playing, learning. I was meant to have them, but I don't fully understand why they chose me."

"Because, like anything I have seen you do since meeting you six months ago, you exceed everyone's expectations." I smile at him.

Alwin pulls me in for a kiss, and then the bright light of day begins to rise. I am highlighting the steady flow of the waterfall. After putting my deck back in my pocket, I pulled the map out and looked at the next spot, but nothing appeared except that the city was marked where the falls were.

"Good morning." Davi's rested voice fills my ears.

"I think we need to head into the falls. Looks like the entrance to the city is through there." I point directly ahead of us.

"Then into the unknown we go," Alwin remarks.

Once we packed and ensured the fire was completely out, we headed to the pool's edge. "We'll need to swim there. I'm unsure how deep the water is, but don't stray from the bank."

My gaze drifted to Davi. "I can swim. A little. Okay, good enough to keep my head above water. Stop worrying about me."

He leaps, and my stomach lurches, watching his entire body submerge. My eyes frantically searched for him to breach, but nothing happened. "I'm going in."

Without another second, Alwin dives headfirst, and I follow.

The water is clear once the wake of our entrance dissipates. I try to find them, but something is pulling me deeper. I kick and scratch towards the surface, but it doesn't work. My lungs burn for air, and I can hear my heart pounding in my ears. Darkness clouds my vision, and I feel it when I'm about to give in.

The burning flame of my phoenix comes to life inside of me. My arm crunches as feathers of flame form on each appendage. Each finger twists until turning into long talons. I can feel my legs shrinking until the firebird takes over my body.

Taking flight, I shoot out of the water, taking to the sky. When I return to the pool, I see the reflection of the most beautiful animal ever. But then my eye catches the dark ribbons of ink spreading through the clear liquid.

Alwin.

I tried to call his name, but my voice didn't sound normal.

A hand breaches the surface, and I glide down, my talons gripping the thick wrist. I flap as hard as I can, their weight increasing the higher out of the water they come. Davi is wrapped in Alwin's arms, taking in deep gulps of air while coughing up water.

"Serena!" Alwin calls to me, and I caw at him. His black eyes meet mine, and we both feel relief. I drag them half-body to the bank and wait until they're safe again before shooting to the sky. I'm looking across as far as I can see. Something flickers in the distance, and I fly towards it. Reaching out, the edge of my claw feels a vibration coming from that part of the sky. I press forward and watch with amazement as it disappears.

False barrier.

With this knowledge, I land and will my figure to transform. Nothing happens. I try to concentrate, but the phoenix has her claws in too deep.

"Serena, what's wrong?" Alwin asks. I come up to his chest and frantically make a noise. "Calm down."

I signal for him to follow me and look over my shoulder as they do. Once we are standing in front of the barrier, I meet his eye, a silent plea to trust me before I fly into it.

ALWIN

A s I try to recover from the traumatic experience of almost
drowning in the powerful waterfalls, I keep my eyes fixed on
the majestic phoenix. Its vibrant colors and graceful
movements leave me in awe as it glides effortlessly toward a wall of
illusion, gradually fading from my view.

"Move it, Puny." I grip the back of his collar and race forward.

Beams of light swirl around as our bodies are lifted from the ground,
transporting through what I can only describe as a tunnel. I keep my
hold tight onto Davi, the pull growing stronger the further we fall.

The sun's light hits my eyes just before we're dropped onto a soft
patch of grass. My grip on Davi falters upon impact as we roll a few
feet. I roll onto my back, blinking away the bright rays before standing.
"Serena! Where are you?"

"She's over there," Davi answers, and I look in the direction he's
pointing. Perched on the silver gate is my firebird. "It's apparent that
her phoenix is still in charge. It must think she's in danger."

The Rune Master has a point, and I think about that as my gaze travels
to the city behind the wall. It's bustling with life past a stone bridge
that runs over a stream of water that matches that of the pool we nearly
drowned in. I approach the gate, reaching out to touch it, when Serena
caws at me. Our eyes meet, and she flaps her wings before gliding over

the entrance.

"What's she doing?" Davi asks.

"A flyover." Because that's exactly what that meant: she could cover more ground faster than we would walk. I push the gate, but nothing happens.

"Perhaps try a password."

"If I wanted your input, Puny, I'd ask." He raises his hands in a signal of defeat. I'm hard on him, but it's because I don't trust him. Serena has a particular affection for him. Her ability to forgive is one thing I'll never be able to do.

While watching from a distance as Serena's form grows smaller the further she flies, an elf dressed in violet armor approaches us with a jagged spear. "What is your business in Silver City?"

My hackles rise. I bare my teeth, but he doesn't appear to be phased by my warning.

"We're just humble travelers looking for a place to stay for the night. If you would be so kind as to show us a fine tavern or inn." Davi's irritating skill at manipulating others into doing something could be in our favor.

"We have a certain disdain for those we deem as threats." His gaze assessesme from head to toe. "Sanctuary is something we grant but only to those in need." he states.

Davi limps forward, gripping his stomach, and it could be partially faked, but I won't say a word to contradict him if it will get us inside. "Let me clarify. We do seek sanctuary within your walls because, you see when we were stranded here three days ago by an evil witch, she left us with no water, and with us not being from here, we nearly died from drinking from the sea."

"You did? Only a child is foolish enough not to know better. Those waters are infested with soul creatures. Their main job is to trap more unfortunate victims in their dark abyss. How did you survive?" The guard seems trapped by the Rune Master's dramatized accounts of what happened. "This big oaf is a Rieke Master?"

I raise a brow and go to speak, but apparently, I have lost my tongue to the annoying man at my side.

"Apprentice. But he picks up on things quicker than most. That's why Master Mikao chose him."

The guard's eyes widened in surprise and admiration. "You work with the legend?"

I laugh on the inside. Master Mikao will find this humorous. Or won't react at all to the humble bastard.

"Why yes, we're close friends with him. If word got back to you, what's your name again?"

"Joana Greyson."

"Right, Guard Greyson was the one who granted us sanctuary in Silver City; the Rieke Master would show his gratitude in some way. With a spiritual healing session or other means."

Greyson looks between us, then at the gate, the city, and with a sigh, removes a key from the ring attached to his belt. It swings open smoother than expected, and he lets us through before securing it again. "Promise me you won't cause problems? King Alistair will have my head if he finds out I helped two enemies into his realm."

Davi laughs, and I scoff, but the severe nature of the guard tells me he's serious. "Oh, definitely not an enemy."

"Right. If you cross the bridge, follow the main path ten buildings down; the Firebird Inn and Tavern is the brick building on the left. You can't miss it, as there's a large phoenix painted across the rooftop."

"Your King has an affection towards the legendary bird?" I ask. "He considers them to be rare signs of fate. If one were ever to cross your path, it would be like looking at a god or goddess." The guard didn't know how close he was to one.

Walking away from the front, I remain quiet, not wanting to praise

Davi for his cleverness. I listen for *her*. Please pay attention to the people we pass, how they dress, and the way they whisper to one another about the newcomers. When we make it to the door, I take one last glance at the skies, hoping to see her. *Where are you, Phoenix?*

"Come, she'll find us." Davi taps me on the shoulder as an old friend and walks inside. I follow, ready for drunks and loud music, but what greets us is surprising. A front area with one person and adjacent to that is a small seating area with four tables all filled with people eating.

"One room? Or two?" the human woman asks.

"One room, two beds." I get out before Davi can even attempt to escape my sight. "We'll take our food in the room."

She nods and hands over a brass key shaped like a firebird. "Up the stairs, last door on the right. Dinner will be brought up in an hour." She sniffs us and wrinkles her nose. "And I'll have them bring you both fresh clothes."

Davi sniffs himself and then coughs. "We smell like shit."

"Worse than that. It smells like you two took a swim in the bog." She states. I tire of the back and forth and trek to the room without another word.

It's one of the most lavish establishments I've ever stayed in. The smell is something like cleaned linen; there's not a speck of dirt to be seen, and aside from the two beds, there are two wardrobes, each with a four-tier candle stick on it. I set my bag down and moved to the bathroom, not caring for Davi's protest to bathe first.

I need to connect with Serena, and the only way I can do that is to find some peace. With the door locked, I strip down and look for the basin to fill, but there's something different about this bathroom. Everything is shiny and looks new. The soaps smell funny but better than my current state.

With the hot water pouring down me, I sit on the floor, cross my legs, and focus on my mate.

"Serena, where are you? Are you safe?" I wait for her to answer, but the longer the silence, the more worried I get.

"Alwin!" Her voice is panicked, and I try to connect with her visually. To make out what she is seeing. Flashes of bars, humans, and elves surround her, a reflection in their armor showing me she's still in her phoenix form. *"He has me. You need to run!"*

"Where are you?" It flashes again, but I can barely make it out.

My ears twitch to listen to what is happening. I can only make out one voice, one name spoken as a face comes into view.

"Now the universe will know that fates favor me, firebird."

"Lord Alistair, what would you have us do?" He smirked, reaching a finger into the cage. *Serena pecks at his finger, drawing blood, but he laughs.*

"Don't let her out of your sight until I return."

My eyes snap open. The rage I feel is boiling inside me; before I know what's happening, my fist connects with the wall, shattering the tile and leaving a hole.

"Alwin? Are you okay? Did you fall?" I push to my feet, leave the shower, not caring it's still on, and grab the towel before entering the main chamber. I dry off quickly, ignoring Davi's presence entirely. "What happened there?"

I find the clean clothes folded neatly on the right wardrobe and quickly put them on, tossing my hair into a high tail at the back of my head.

"Um, hello, you're bleeding." It takes his touch on my wrist to remember where we are. My hand around his throat as a growl vibrates in my throat. "Dark One, snap out of it!"

I blink a few times, the red color of rage clearing my vision, and release him. The Rune Master is heaving and gasping for air.

"They have her. He has her." I say, swiping a hand down my face. "Who?" He croaks, standing.

"Alistair. He's got her…" I pause, my fists curling at my sides. "In a cage."

30

"Fuck. Alright, I'll get ready, and we can go." Davi heads to the bathroom, but I don't have time to waste on him.

Looking at my bleeding knuckles, I grab a spare towel and quickly wrap it before pulling my sack on my back and heading out the door.

I need to secure a weapon first, which may prove more difficult than I anticipated, being that I'm a stranger here and the greeting at the gate doesn't give me any hope that they'd be willing to sell one to me.

"I see my son's clothes fit you well." The woman who gave me the key catches my attention as I pass her.

Looking down, I see I'm wearing all black, the shirt and pants fitting me well. "Yes. Thank you."

"Are you in a hurry?" I furrow my brows. "You look like you're making a quick exit. Something wrong with the room?"

"No." I approached her. "I just need to find an armorer or a blacksmith."

She clears her throat. "Why?"

"Are you always invested in your customers' business?" "When they want to seek a weapon, yes." I hum, and she

elaborated, "Vwriynn, the main island, was destroyed because of strangers with access to weapons. King Alistair has made Silver City a safe place for anyone to live, and there are rules we must follow. To include no weapons. There is no need for any. The guards have them, but that's to protect us. I'll have to report you."

"I wouldn't." I snarl.

She smiles. "Or you could tell me why you're here."

This woman is old, but something about her tells me she isn't messing around. "I don't take it kindly to be blackmailed."

"And I'm just trying to ensure you're not here to cause trouble." She backfires.

"I'm looking for someone." You might as well start with a half- truth. "She's critical to me and the person who took her. Well, he isn't unarmed,

31

and I fear the only way I can get her back is with force."

"I see." She rubs her chin. "If she is in the city's gates, you must report it to the Watch. They'll be able to help you locate her."

I shake my head from side to side. "No. I know where she is. It's getting her back that's the issue."

"And you think this will be resolved with violence?" "If need be," I reply under my breath.

She sighs. "Give me a reason to trust you, and I might be able to help you out."

How can I convince a stranger to trust me? As if the fates are on my side, I hear Davi walk beside me, freshly showered and dressed in new clothes.

"And I see my daughter's clothes fit you well." the woman comments, and I laugh. Davi scowls but then thanks her. "I suppose you'll be seeking a weapon as well?"

"Me? No. But I see my friend has told you why he needs one?" Davi responds.

"He was just getting to the part about convincing me not to report you both." she states with a judgmental eye on me.

Davi reaches out and touches her arm; simultaneously, I see him dig into his rune bag. "You can trust us." I feel magic in the air as a ringing sound briefly hits my ears. The woman's eyes widened, and then Davi let her go. She pulls out a parchment and ink pen, scribbles something down, and then digs her pocket for something.

"Take this and go here. Ask for Cordelia." I look down and see the name of a building. A golden coin decorated with a firebird sits on top of it.

"Thank you." Davi nods and then grabs the stuff before guiding me outside.

When we're far enough away, I go to ask what he did, but he speaks before I can.

"A small Rune Master trick."

"Though they were just for portal-ling?" "And that's why they never chose you." "Care to explain further?"

"No, Dark One. Some secrets of the Runes are more important than any threat you could ever give me."

I can respect him for that.

We approach the building, and they all look the same, except this one has a golden phoenix carved into the door. I knock three times, and the eyehole slides open. "We request a visit with Cordelia."

The piece slams back into place, the locks turn, and the door opens. We walk inside, and then a chill runs up my spine. My vision changes to see through the pitch black, but at the last second, I see someone coming at me with a large log; I catch their wrist, but don't see the one behind me as pain erupts in the back of my head before I fall forward. Davi's limp body lies opposite mine, and my vision fades as unconsciousness envelops me.

SERENA

As a little girl, I watched the Bird keeper across the path feed and sell different kinds of food. The prettiest ones were the blue jays and cardinals. Their feathers would shine brightly when the sun would hit them to ride. I always wanted to run my hand across them. One day, I ventured out alone when no one was watching. There was a cage at my eye level, and I reached inside. The feathers felt better than I imagined in my head. Smooth, silky, and clean.

They made the bleakness of Narborim fade away for a few minutes. At that moment, I wasn't a half-elf girl trapped in the isolation of her rotting house. I was just a girl petting a bird in those few stolen minutes.

And then that moment ended.

The Bird keeper reached my wrist and clamped down as hard as she could before tossing me into the mud. I was scared, humiliated, and trapped. That's how I feel right now. Caught in the clutches of an elf who believes I'm a gift from the fates. Aside from his president ogling from the other side of these iron bars, his intentions are unknown.

I don't understand why I haven't changed back. The mind-numbing thought has been running on repeat since it happened. I'm not sure how this happened, or why I can't seem to control the essence inside of me, but I'm starting to fear that I may never transfigure again.

Alwin! I call through our bond. *Please give me a sign that you are still connected with me.* I reached out to him. Our tether strained from the distances and iron separating us. Even with all my fire- power, I feel cold without him, like a wall of ice blocking me from getting to him.

The door to the room creaks open on its hinges, and in comes to my captor. Alistair McCain, King of Silver City. That's how he introduced himself to me when the net shot into the sky took me down. His hair is trimmed short above his pointed ears, and his eyes are blue grey, almost like Alwin's. He has a beard and mustache, the color of snow. Come to think of it, he looks nearly identical to Alwin aside from his age.

"Hello, firebird," he greets me with a smile, a tiny piece of meat pinched between his finger and thumb. I eye it, but nothing about it seems to be appetizing. "You must be hungry after flying here from the outer realms. Where do the fates reside?"

I don't acknowledge him. Turning my beak up at the raw food he's trying to feed me. Closing my eyes, I focus on returning to my regular form. Nothing happens, and I don't know why. What happened between jumping in that pool and breaking the surface?

"When you're hungry, truly starving, you'll eat whatever I give you." He sighs, tosses the meat onto a plate, and picks up a vine of grapes. Their vibrant purple color and fruity scent make my mouth water. An involuntary noise escapes me, echoing through the room, and he smiles. Juices from his half-eaten food dripped down his chin. "A fruit lover? Very well." He presents it to me, and I greedily peck one off the vine. "Good. Eat. You'll need to refuel your energy before I suggest you to the people. They've worshiped you for decades.

"Did you know you're a legend around here? An inspiration to my citizens. That's why you see the phoenix painted everywhere." I swallow the pieces of grape, look around for something to drink, and notice a small bowl of water. We continue to share the delicious fruit while he rambles about why I'm here and what it means to this city. "I've been around for a few centuries, Firebird. When I learned about you, your power, and the endless possibilities that your existence could mean, I vowed to myself that if I ever saw you, I'd make you mine. That's why I invented the perfect cage.

These bars," he said, gripping one while putting the empty vine down, "are not just made with pure iron.

"It's infused with the essence of two tarot cards." Alistair digs into his pocket and pulls out a deck. He was shouting at them while keeping his eyes squarely on me. "The thing that non-tarot masters don't know is how powerful these painted parchments are. Each one has power of their own. You can't control exactly what they gift you with, but they learn from you after many years of bonding. Your mind, body, and soul." He stops shuffling and pulls the top two cards, revealing them to me without looking at them.

"*The Chariot* and *The Hermit*. Both have multiple meanings, but know I needed to level up this cage and the net used to bring you down." That's how these items are so powerful. I can't feel my essence at all. "And that's why you aren't in your true form." I caw at him, asking him to elaborate and question how he knows I'm not a bird. He gives me a pearly white smile. "Yes, Firebird, I know what you are. Inside that fire-feathered bodice is a two-legged being ready to break free. That won't happen until I let you out of this cage." My wings flap, trying to get him to understand that is precisely what I want.

Alistair laughs, pushes to his feet, and puts his cards back into his pocket. "Don't fret; I will free you once I know why you're here. Then, when you agree to stand by my side as my Queen, you'll be presented to the people in whatever being you are. Elf, human, dwarf, it makes no difference to me." The doors to the chamber swing open, revealing a man who seems to be a guard.

"My Lord, I apologize for the interruption, but there have been reports of two strangers wandering around the Front Market." the Guard states.

"This place is a sanctuary, and you know my policy. They're meant to be here if they make it through the barrier." Alistair responds.

"Of course. It's just they're here inquiring about purchasing weapons." Alistair rubs his beard at this. "And..."

The Shadow King approaches the guard, giving him his full attention. "Spit it out."

"One appears to have the same essence as you, My Lord." "Who says this?" he asks.

The Guard's eyes darted to me and then back to his king. My chest tightens as I try to diffuse the rampant thoughts racing through my head. Alwin wouldn't use his powers openly if he thought it wasn't safe. I don't believe Davi is foolish enough to reveal who he is. But as the saying goes, whatever fate decides is already set in stone. "She did. The innkeeper."

Alistair seems to ponder this momentarily before nodding. "And these two have been subdued?"

"She sent them to *her*."

"Very well. Have them brought to the cells." Alistair turns on his heel and approaches me. His eyes narrow as a smile breaks free before he says, "Something tells me you didn't come alone, Firebird. Don't worry; you'll see your companions again." By the sinister look reflecting in his eyes, I try to call upon my power, but a bucket of numbing balm has been poured all over me. My wings flap frantically as my chest tightens, and the screeching tearing through my throat causes tears in my eyes.

The rest of the day went on slowly, leaving me thinking of endless terrible possibilities. I attempted to transform through the bleak loneliness multiple times, but nothing happened.

My powers are failing me.

I only lifted my head when Alistair came waltzing inside with a trail of people following him. Servants, guards, other members of his court, and then finally, two men, bagged and bounded, were ushered inside. I knew the instant I saw the tall one that it was him. He was here. Alive and appearing unharmed.

Alwin and Davi were forced to the marble floor; Alistair took his throne, the impact of their knees resounding in my ears. Two women, wearing a silver mask covering their faces aside from their eyes and nose, stood at either side. They were dressed in pure skintight clothing matching the color of their mask.

I looked around the room, memorizing each face I could so that if any harm came to my mate, I'd know who to turn into ash. "The trial for the two trespassers has begun." one of the guardsmen spoke.

"Tall one," Alistair started pointing at Alwin, although he couldn't see through the bag over his eyes. "Remove the bag."

The woman on Alwin's right does as ordered. I watch him blink at the brightest, his hair falling across his shoulders. Something that resembled the color of blood coating his forehead. I squinted to see better, and my fire came alive when I did.

Each head turned to me. My rage and flames burning through the bars echoed around the room. I could see the bars beginning to bend against my essence. So I didn't stop.

No matter the terror I was causing. No matter what Alistair would do.

The only thought coursing through my head was that they hurt my mate, and now they have to pay.

"The Phoenix, it's melting the bars." someone said. "Not possible. They're pure iron." another responded. The fright in their voices only fueled me further.

Good. Be afraid of me. Fear my power.

I push and push as the metal begins to melt. Each drop brings me closer to freedom. A shadow comes over me; two dark hands grip the bars and pull them together.

"No!" It comes out in my normal voice. "It's a she-elf." one of the guards exclaims.

I look down, seeing that I'm standing on two feet, my body draped in a dress of gold and crimson flames. Wings of fire burn brightly at my back while fire sprays from my palms. My eyes lock with Alistairs as the fight for control continues. I snarled, and he sneered, sweat beading across his brow.

"Kill them!" he commands.

"Stop!" I scream, my gaze cutting to the two men kneeling on the floor. Alwin's eyes meet mine, and a blade comes across his neck. His body falls to the floor, blood pooling around him. Those eyes that ensnared mine every time we made love, blinking, his soul fading. "Murderer."

My essence tears through me in an explosion of flames and light, knocking everyone into the walls and causing debris to fall from the ceiling. All I see is red.

I lock eyes with the woman in silver closest to Alwin and approach her. She stands with a blade in hand, her bright eyes revealing no fear, and I catch the subtlest movement beneath her mask. She's mocking me with a smile.

I don't give her mercy. Pointing one finger at her, I let my fire go, but she dodged and struck my neck. My shield of heat burns her hand, and she screams, stumbling backward. This time, I see it. The fear and it's intoxicating.

"You should've never touched my mate." I snarl before igniting the spot where she stood, my fire consuming her body, screams, mind, and soul. A single sound resounded throughout the hall when the hilt hit the floor. Beside it, a pile of ash.

"Serena." I hear Davi call my name and turn to him. His bindings are free, his bag removed, and his eyes widened, a mix of admiration and trepidation shining back at me.

"Did they hurt you?" I ask him. He shakes his head from side to side. Then I look over to the Shadow King, the pads of my feet leaving a trail of cinders in the floor. He stands before me, his deck of cards out in preparation to fight me. But he doesn't know I have my essence of tarot ready to defend me.

"Pheonix, I meant no harm. If you let me, I can heal him, but I must move quickly." Alistair pleads. The taunting and belittling tone from earlier was replaced with terror.

"If you're lying to me, you will join my mate in the afterlife," I warn, and he nods his understanding.

Alistair moves swiftly, rushing over to Alwin's limp body. He does exactly what I saw my mate do with Davi—touching his heart and forehead. Incoherent words pass his lips, and I watch, pleading with the fates to not take him from him. We've been separated for far too long.

Golden light shines under his palms, and the hum of magic dances in the air between us. I watched and waited for hours, which were only minutes. My attention was solely on his chest. When it finally rose, relief and tears flooded me. I raced to his side, lifting his cold hand to mine and kissing it. Brushing the hair from his face, I saw him blink a few times before he fell into a deep sleep.

"He'll sleep for a day or two. I had to pull him from the edge." Alistair explained. "I will set you up in guest chambers."

Alistair attempted to move, but I swiftly grabbed him by the neck. My sharpened nails sank into his skin as I lifted him off the ground while pushing myself to my feet. His feet dangled in front of me, hands desperately scratching at my arm, urging me to release him. "You ordered him to die. We came here for help, but your first instinct was imprisoning us. No one touches him without paying the price."

Something deep inside of me that I didn't know was there rose its head up. I latched onto it. A branch contacted me from my ancestor's past, showing me this was the right thing to do. This was the power of the true Phoenix, and to use it only when necessary because it can't be undone once I do this.

"Phoenix, please!" I saw my reflection shining in him. My flames consumed my body aside from the hand around his throat.

"You've abused the gifts you were given, and now, I shall take them away." Inhaling deeply, I pushed the essence into him, whispering the spell of undoing, "Has ego potestates a te."

Alistair's screams of pain are far off in the distance as I feel the shadows leaving him. I was detached from his soul, dissipating against the light of my flames. It's alarming and empowering. His body slumps over, and I let him fall to the floor.

"What did you do to him?" Davi asks, his voice low with caution.

"I did the only thing worse than death." Davi looked at me as I stared into the Rune Masters's face and continued, "I burned the essence from his soul. The Shadow King is no more."

"You mean he's non-magic?" Davi asks, and I nod. "Oh, my fates."

"Alistair is still a tarot master in skill, but he has no power of the cards in his pocket. He can no longer command the power of healing through Rieke. So, yes, Davi, he has no more magic." I explained.

A groan came from Alistair as he struggled to his feet. I was immediately looking smaller than when I first laid eyes upon him. "You... you bitch. How could you? After I saved him."

"You killed him. And so many others." I responded, uncaring what insult he would come up with next.

"For someone who loves the ancient firebird so much, you know so little about her true power. And messing with her mate was the dumbest thing anyone could ever do." Davi said to the King. "Now, what should we do with the rest of them?"

I turned to face the crowd, all paralyzed with fear at my feet. "You may all return home. There is nothing left for you here."

"All except you two." Davi pointed to the other woman in silver and another dressed in black and brown leather. The two fell on their knees at my feet.

"Go home," I commanded; they looked at me confused at first, but then scrambled to their feet and took off out the door.

"Why?"

"Davi, shut it. Or you will need to find the next Rune Master before your time is up."

ALWIN

"I still don't know how she did that." I hear Davi's hushed tones as I blink away the brain fog.

My neck is sore, and I swore I could remember dying. I sit up slowly and examine the room I'm in. Davi is in the corner speaking with no one? Or himself? I'm not sure, but that doesn't matter because I'm no longer chained, nor is he. No bars surround us, but one thing doesn't make sense.

"Where is she?" I hoarsely ask. I rub my neck and try to clear my throat. Davi turns to me, stuffing something like his Runes back inside his pocket before walking over to me and picking up a cup of water. "What happened?"

"You died. Serena saved us. Killed the lady in silver that slit your throat and then burned Alistair's essence from his soul." I blink three times to ensure I'm no longer sleeping. "Your mate is powerful. More so than anyone has ever known since the first Phoenix walked the universe."

Did she burn his essence? Not possible. "Where is she? What do you mean I died? How am I sitting here talking to you if that were the case?" I sip on more water, slowly trying to calm the aching in my throat. Each word feels like I'm dragging nails across my windpipe.

He sighs. "Serena is waiting in the throne hall for you."

43

Immediately, I stand. Initially, I am a little dizzy, but I brush that off and move towards the door. "Alwin," Davi's concern makes me pause as I turn the handle and look at him over my shoulder. "There is something different about her since we came here."

"It's been a day; how much could she have changed since the last sunrise?" I don't wait for him to answer, and I take my leave of him. At first, I noticed how lost I was until a guard pointed me in the right direction. If that isn't daunting, I'm not sure what is.

"Dark One," another guard bows, and I'm unsure what else to do.

"The Phoenix Queen is waiting for you." another states, escorting me down a narrow corridor and through an arched open doorway that leads directly into the throne room. The last place I remember seeing her alive, behind bars in her firebird form.

As I walk in, my breath is caught at the sight before me. There is no longer a trapped bird in a cage but my beautiful mate, sitting on a throne of flames with a dress made of fire covering her. Her hair is braided in two, the tails just brushing her navel. I swallow down the lump in my throat and make my way to her. She catches sight of me and is instantly on her feet, soon in my arms.

Her fiery scent engulfs, but her flames do not. "Alwin." "Serena, what happened? Puny said some crazy stuff, but I'd rather hear from you." She pulls back from me, her hands cupping my face as she pulls me in for a deep kiss. Our tongues collide in heat and passion. Her hands move to the hem of my shirt, ripping it from me as my back hits a wall. "Fuck now, talk later."

My hands skim her body, the flames disappearing to reveal her naked form to me. "It's been too long, my mate."

Serena pulls my pants to my ankles, my cock springs free, and she wraps her long fingers around my shaft, pumping me up and down as I devour her mouth. My shadows come to life as my mate bond

44

recognizes her. I run my fingers through her soaking pussy and insert two fingers, pumping before moving my hands to her hips and lifting her so she can wrap her legs around me. My tip nudged at her entrance, and in one move, I thrust inside of her, making us both moan.

Our foreheads press together for a brief moment before I spin us, pushing her into the wall and pumping in and out of her at a fast pace. I feel her nails raking down my back as my tongue trails the length of her neck. "Alwin." she moans my name, which awakens my need for her.

"Serena." I capture her lips as I palm her breast with one hand and use the other to tease her bundle of nerves that I know makes her go crazy. My mouth waters to taste her. I lean forward after moving my hands back to support her hips and claim each nipple. Nibbling until I swirl my tongue around them and sucking until I leave my mark. She begins to clench around me, and I know she's close to her first climax.

I capture her mouth with mine again and move one hand to her clit, pinching and rubbing until finally, she squeezes my cock, moaning my name. She opens her eyes, looking at me with all the love I feel for her, reflecting on me. Her feet are lower to the ground, but I'm not done with her yet. I pull out, then lift her into my arms, carrying her to her new seat of power.

"They call you the Phoenix Queen." I sit down; she positions herself in front of me with her back to me, then sinks. I pull her back to me, my arm across her chest, and the other snakes around her waist. Her wings of flames are gone; just like any additional time, I touch her from behind. "I always knew you were a Queen, Serena. Mine, and right now, I'm going to fuck you on this throne while you scream my name so this entire city knows exactly who you belong to."

I don't wait for her response as I move in and out of her, our bodies building sweat and my pace speeding with each thrust. I sink my teeth into the side of her neck, causing her head to fall back against my shoulder and her nails to dig into my thighs. Every pleasure I give her matches the small pinches of pain she brings me. Serena is my mate, and I can only consider pleasing her. Feeling her pussy clench down and milking me until her womb is filled with my seed.

"Alwin," she moans, and I move the hand from her chest to her mouth; she sucks on my fingers, and I groan, pumping faster. I'm getting close as I feel my balls seizing up, but I know she needs to climax with me. I gag her, then use my hand around her waist to move to her clit and rub until I feel her orgasm building.

"Now, Serena," I command, and with her teeth biting into my fingers, she brings us both over the edge; I spill my seed into her as she clenches down around me through her climax. We sit there for a few heartbeats, our bodies relaxing as we come down from our high.

I trace my fingers up and down her back, causing gooseflesh to rise, and she sighs. I'm unsure if she's ready to talk, but I know she will once she's ready. Serena interlaces her fingers with my free hand and brings the back of my hand up to her lips for a soft kiss. "Alwin, there are some things I need to tell you."

"I know, Firebird. When you're ready." I assure her.

"Let's get cleaned up, and then we will talk." After untangling ourselves from one another, I redress, and she covers her body in those flames again. I watch as she moves over to a table and pours liquid from a decanter into two cups, handing one to me. She seems nervous, and I hate that she feels this way when it's just the two of us.

"Tell me, Serena. Nothing you can say will keep me from you." She flashes a half-smile and begins.

I listened to every detail from beginning to end, starting from when she went through the wall to when I was taken to the infirmary. "And it just clicked when I saw your soul leaving your eyes. A well of power overflowing as a damn that was blocking it burst open. It was unlike anything I'd ever seen or felt before. I heard ancient ones speaking inside my head, filling it with different spells and visions of past phoenixes.

When I killed that woman, I could see nothing but red. Every thought that passed through my head was turning her to ask for what she did to you. Then, when I faced Alistair, the man who is the reason we're here, the reason that child was dead, and who captured me, I knew what I had to do."

Her eyes met mine in a flash of worry. She was afraid to confirm what Davi had told me. I reached for her, and she didn't shy away, allowing me to pull her close to comfort her emotions, guilt, shame, or power.

"Tell me what you did, Firebird." She lowered her chin, but I lifted it, keeping my gaze locked. "I know saying it out loud will make it real to you, but I need to hear it, and so do you."

Tears swelled in her eyes, and I could see it. The turmoil she was feeling for what she had done. What she had taken from another like us. "I burned... I burned his essence from him, making him a nonmagic."

I wiped each tear from her cheer before reassuring her, "You did what you thought was right, Serena. There is no shame in that."

"I'm a monster, Alwin." She backs away from me, looking at her hands like poisonous vipers ready to strike. "This power inside of me, it's dark."

"But it's also light." I step towards her, but she halts me with her hand up. I keep forcing her until her back is against the wall, the tips of her toes are brushing my boots, and our chests are rubbing against one another. "You're my mate, Serena, and I'm called the Dark One. The darkness inside you is part of the balance of our bond." I pull my shirt aside to reveal our imprint. My shadow swirls, dancing around her phoenix form. "You were born from the light, and I from the dark. Our bond gives us the equilibrium we both need to survive. Neither one of us is tipping the scale in either direction." I'm so close to her now; our breath mingles, and her scent is washing over me. The smell of our mixed cum was still strong inside of her. "You saw me die, that made the scale lean to the shadows, and you discovered a new gift. And to me, it is one because now we have a secret weapon that can be used to defeat not only Queen Lilac but also the Amazon Queen. Those two thrive on their ability to use essence."

"Because death is too good for the likes of them." she whispers. "That's right, Firebird." I wink, and that coaxes a smile out of her. "Keep that smile, Serena. Don't let anything or anyone take that from you." I lean down and kiss her. I am pouring all my strength and love for her into it because that's what she needs from me. And I realized long ago that I would do anything for her. Be anyone to her because she is my fate; she will be the next Queen of this universe, and I'll be right by her side. If not only for her to mate with but as a weapon for her to use at her will.

Someone clears their throat, causing us to break apart, and I roll my eyes as Puny's scent fills my nose. We both turn to look at him. "Sorry to interrupt, but he's asking for you."

"Alistair. You have him locked away?" I ask her.

"Seemed only right to do to him what he did to me. Powerless and behind bars." She shrugs, and I smirk, can't help but feel pride swell in my chest. "Bring him here or have the guards do it. I think it's time for Alistair, the former Shadow King, to meet the new one."

She links her hand with mine, walking me over to the throne before taking a seat. I stand over her right shoulder, keeping a protective arm across her chest. Not that she needs it.

* * *

Alistair looks strikingly familiar to me. Only he has white hair on his head and face. He's kneeling before us, and Serena looks him over a few times before signaling Puny to let him speak.

"I see the throne suites you." He croaks out.

"What do you want, Alistair?" Serena asks, sounding annoyed. "A pardon or a chance to work on an alliance with you and your

mate." He points to me but doesn't look at me. He appears to be afraid to meet my eye. This could be due to his weakened state now that he is no more than a nonmagic elf.

"There's nothing you could offer me except for your head.

Which I'm still inclined to take. I need it to free someone very dear to me." That catches my attention. She doesn't feel threatened if she reveals that to him.

"So, your purpose for coming here was an assassination?" He accuses.

"My purpose for coming here would've been friendly if you hadn't captured first and asked questions later." Serena snaps. "Give me one reason why I should keep you alive. Your people have welcomed me as their new Queen within less than the sunrise I've sat on this throne. Your armies and guards pledge their loyalty to me and every council member. What could you possibly offer me?"

Alistair's eyes cut around the room as he looks for the answer on one of the walls. "I used Reiki to heal him. There are so few masters left in the universe. I can teach you." He spits out.

"Without your essence, the ritual is useless. I have no desire to become a healer." she retorts. Alistair fumbles for another answer.

"What about shadow magic? There are things your mate doesn't know I could teach him."

I answer this time, "There's nothing that I don't know, old man." "Be that as it may, I'm still older than you, boy." This time, our

eyes lock, and I get a clear view of his face. I study it while he continues to ramble on about training me in ways my father taught me—an image of when I was six years old flashes in my head. A man is standing next to my father; they're identical twins, but this one has a scar across his right cheek. I return to the present, and my feet move on their own accord as I close the distance between him and me. When I reach him, I lift him, brushing my fingers through his beard until I feel the uneven skin.

"How did you get that?" I ask.

"What? None of your business, and put me down." He snaps. "Where are you from? Did you have a twin?" The questions pour

out of me as I realize who this man is to me. "Was your brother Alfred?"

His eyes widen at the mention of my father's name. "How do you know that name?"

"Answer my questions first." I challenged him before dropping him to the floor.

"Alwin, do you know him?" Serena asks.

Alistair's eyes meet mine as he rubs the spot on his cheek before standing. "My older brother gave me this scar when we were children. It was during a dagger training session, and he went too far. Of course, my father never stepped in to stop him until he saw the blood."

Fuck.

"We can't kill him," I whisper to my mate. "He's my uncle."

SERENA

A fter the revelation in the throne hall, we retired to the dining hall and had food brought in so Alistair could reconnect with his nephew, who hadn't seen him in over two centuries. I keep forgetting how old Alwin is compared to me, but he was never half-human.

"Alfred, damn him, kept me from you when I tried to stop him from following down your grandfather's path," Alistair said between sips of water. "He wanted to make you unbeatable mind and body like we were. Then, when the time came for me to stop him, I was banished here to Vwriynn. There was nothing here but what you've seen. I came to this small, secluded island and made it mine. Slowly returning to the mainland to find any locals I could that were willing to help me build Silver City, and in return, I grant them sanctuary."

Fuck, he sounds like a saint now.

"Who taught you to be a Tarot Master? And where did you learn Reiki? As far as I know, Master Mikao is the only Master alive." Alwin stated.

Alistair smiled at the mention of the Reiki Master. "Well, I've had a few run-ins with Master Mikao. He's taught me a few tricks here and there because I needed something to teach the people within these walls if we were going to thrive. The tarot, that's something different." He

51

pauses, reflecting, and I can see sadness and fondness mixing in his eyes. "I had a teacher, and his name was Master Runk. He was human, honest, and very in tune with his cards. Every time he spoke about one, it was as if he was reading it from one of the ancient scrolls. He passed down everything he knew, including his deck, to me before he passed."

Now, I feel humiliated. What was I thinking?

Alwin must've sensed my distress and placed a calming hand on my thigh.

"Do not fret, Phoenix Queen, you taking my essence from me is not the end of the world. I have many talents, as I told you, that can be useful to all of us. Including the Puny one." I chuckled at using Alwin's nickname for Davi as we watched him scarf down a chicken thigh. "What role does he play in this little trio?"

"Puny is a Rune Master." I answered.

"A Master of Runes, how rare a find. There is great honor in your practice." Alistair says to Davi, who has just finished swallowing a mouthful.

"Thank you." he responds.

"Now that we're all being honest with one another, why don't you start telling me why you are here?" Alistair asked before biting into a piece of bread.

I look at Alwin, who nods for me to take charge. "To make an incredibly long story short, the Amazon Queen has captured our friends, and the only way to get them back is by bringing your head to her."

"I see." He hums, his lips pressing against the rim of his cup. "We weren't going to. We plan to ask you for your allegiance in

the fight against her and Queen Lilac of Xora." Alwin added. "Uncle, is there anything you can tell us about her? How do you fight her and win? My powers are useless against her."

The three of us wait while Alistair ponders his response. "I have a way, but without my essence, it's pointless."

"Tell us, and we can figure out something." I plead.

"You," he points to me, "must pardon me and grant me permission to stay here, seeing this is my home."

"Done," I state.

"You." He points to Davi, "need to power up every Rune you have. I can get you whatever ingredients you need aside from dragon bone. That is very hard to come by." Davi acknowledges him, and then he moves on to Alwin. "You, my dear nephew, must return to Master Mikao and become his apprentice. The only way for us to be ready is if one of us has the power to heal the other."

"Leave here? Without my mate? No." Alwin states, crossing his arms.

"Fine. Bring him here; I'm sure Serena knows how to summon a portal using the Moon Card." At the mention of using my cards, I look away. He doesn't know I'm not a master, not even a novice. "I see. She doesn't know how the cards work. I can train her, but it will take time. For now, I will work on helping you learn one card that will help free your friends. The Devil card will be the one we focus on. Since your Rune Master can summon portals, we should be all set in about two weeks."

"Two weeks? But Niya and Rose may not have that." I protest. "Is there another Tarot Master or apprentice we could call upon

within this realm?" Alwin asks.

Alistair shakes his head from side to side. "I'm not saying it will take that long for Serena to learn how to work with the card, but it may take that long for your Rune Master to restore his blank tiles. Especially since getting access to dragon bones means a portal link to Xora, the only known dragon colony."

"I may have a way of getting it faster," Alwin states, and I grip his wrist.

"Are you sure?"

"Braxor and I have a pact." he responds.

53

"Then it's settled. Alwin will work with getting the dragon's bone here while Davi begins getting the ingredients ready for the restoration spell, and Serena and I will begin our training. Oh, and Alwin will need to have Master Mikao come here." Alistair sounds more pleased with himself than we are feeling now.

* * *

Back in our chambers, shown to us by Alistair, I fluff a pillow before walking over to the wardrobe and looking at the emptiness inside. A sigh escapes me, but the smell of bathing oils has me perking up as I feel Alwin's heat pressing against my back. His teeth nipped at my ear, and our naked bodies pressed together.

"We'll have new clothes brought to you tomorrow." he whispers. "Although, I do approve of flames or nothing at all."

I turn in his arms, my smile faltering. "I didn't have to take his powers."

"Don't do that to yourself."

"But it's true. If he had his essence, we wouldn't need to worry about me training to become a novice Tarot reader." I sigh and lean into his bare chest, soaking in his presence.

He grips my hand and walks me to the bathing chamber. There's a tub big enough for both of us to fit comfortably. I nuzzle in between his legs, his half-erected cock digging into my back. Alwin lathers his hands in oils and presses his fingers into my back muscles. I begin to relax, closing my eyes and letting him take control of my body.

"Are you ready for your coronation tomorrow?" he asks, and my eyes pop open.

"What? When was that discussed?"

"When you left the table, Alistair informed me that for you to become Queen of this realm truly, there needs to be a ceremony, which must happen quickly. He knows you were bluffing about the loyalty of his armies and guards. He thinks having the ceremony tomorrow will ensure they pledge themselves to you."

"I don't deserve nor want to be anyone's Queen." I sigh. "You're mine already, Firebird. And I think it's wise to take

control when offered. We need more power to fight a war against Queen Lilac's armies." He's right, of course.

"If I am Queen, what does that make you?" His fingers stopped, and I feared I may have insulted him, but then he shuffled behind me, making water splash, and I went to turn, and what I saw had my breath catching momentarily. "Alwin, is that?"

"I know the timing may not be right, but we've already accepted each other as mates, and I figured this could be the next step." In his hand is a gilded ring with phoenix wings and an obsidian stone at the center. "Serena Ozark, will you do me the honor of becoming my wife?"

My eyes drifted between the ring and my mate, and as I said, "With all my heart, Alwin, I will marry you."

He slides the ring on my left finger, and I wrap my arms around him, our lips meeting as I straddle him. "Is this truly what you want? For us to become Queen and King of a realm we're not from nor familiar with?"

Alwin's hands rest on my hips under the water, and he looks at me. "As long as we do it together, there isn't anything I wouldn't do with you, Firebird."

"So, we have a plan?" I ask.

"Indeed, we do. You become a Tarot Master, I a Reike Apprentice, and Puny will restore his pieces of rock to portal us back to Whitfrost to save Niya and Rose. Until then," he pauses, then I feel his cock twitching beneath me. "I intend to spend every moment I can worshiping you as my Queen." He lines his tip to my entrance and pushes me down onto him in one move. "My wife." He thrusts, and my head falls back in pleasure. "My mate."

I let him remain in control, his mouth, tongue, teeth, and cock bringing me to my first orgasm. Alwin thrust inside of me, his grip on my hips hard enough to bruise as I kept my grip on his shoulders, our tongues dancing while I rode him. One of his hands finds my clit, and he rubs it just like until I'm clenching down on him. "Alwin."

"Serena." He moans, capturing my left nipple and teasing it between his teeth. "Fuck, I can't wait to taste all of you."

Then he stands, bringing me with him. He walks us over to a bench where our towels are hanging over, sets me, then kneels between my legs, lifting each one so my knees are aligned with his shoulders, giving him the perfect access to my pussy. Alwin runs his tongue over the center, causing me to shiver, and I grip his hair. His fingers tease my inner thighs while he sucks and licks, his tongue diving into my soaking entrance, and I begin to move against it, riding him shamelessly.

Two of his fingers move inside of my pussy while the other explores my ass. A territory we have yet to talk about but one I'm willing to go to with him. "Alwin."

"Only if you wish to." I nod, and he begins to prep it with my previous orgasm. With his mouth on my clit, he has two fingers pumping me in and out while the third still nudges slowly. He inches forward, and there's a burn, but I can take it. Alwin goes to his knuckle and picks up pace before beginning to add a second finger to my ass. My body is stretched, and I'm on the verge of climax again. "Ride my fingers, Firebird. Make yourself cum."

His words lit a fire inside me, and I did as he said. Taking control, riding his fingers while he sucks on my clit, and I feel my orgasm building until I release it. Clenching down hard on him and moaning his name. I don't get time to relax before the hunger in- side of me has me pouncing on him. He falls to the floor, and I straddle him, sinking, and I fuck him. My nails dig into his chest as I move up and down, bringing us both to oblivion. When he's done spilling his seed inside of me, I get off and lick him clean before crawling up to him and kissing him.

We lay on the cold floor for a few minutes before returning to the bath to clean ourselves. I use my fire heat to dry us entirely before we get into our bed, neither of us caring about being naked. Alwin wraps his arms around me, his hand resting on my belly while the other is under the pillow where I have my head. An image of our future comes to mind and has my thoughts buzzing with possibilities. I'm afraid to voice one, but not because of the reasons any bride would have.

"Tell me what's on your mind, Firebird." "Trying to read my thoughts?" I tease.

"You can let me in if it would make it easier." He suggests, and I let my mental walls down, sending him the images and words I won't voice. "One day, when our world is safe, I will gladly fill your womb with our children. A Prince or Princes of shadow fire would be a force this world won't be ready for."

I turn to face him, my heart growing more prominent at the thought of being a mother to his children someday. I cup his cheek, press a chaste kiss to his lips, and look deep into his eyes as I say with all the truth and courage I can muster, "I don't want to wait, Alwin. Tomorrow night, I want to start trying to be a mother. It would never prevent me from doing my duty to this world or the next. I am to be your wife, a Queen, and even if I become with child, I know they will be safe inside of me when the day comes for us to go to war."

Alwin looks at me and smiles, then rolls on top of me nudging my thighs apart. "Why wait another night?"

I laugh. "Have you not had enough of me?"

"Never, Firebird. I'll remove the spell of contraception, right," he closes his eyes, and I can feel the magic coming from him. "Now." He reaches down and lines his tip up to me. I thought I'd be sore, but I'm not there, and he pushes inside of me. "Once I spill my seed in you, that's it. There is no turning back. You will become with child. Are you sure you want this?"

I don't hesitate to answer him, "Yes, Alwin."

Our lips meet only instead of the lust-filled hunger from earlier; it's slow and full of love. As is the rest of the night. As we begin a new chapter, we make love under ribbons of fire and shadow. In nine months, a child of Shadowfire will be born.

✳ ✳ ✳

The following day, I was busy preparing for the ceremonies tonight: a wedding and a coronation taking place all at once. Alistair had brought clothes that fit my new status, but he also added some shirts and pants, knowing I would only wear dresses during ceremonies. Or I assume that's what Alwin told him.

There would be no training for me today. Davi was already working hard with the Royal Apothecary, letting the restoration spell start. Alwin went off privately to contact Braxor and hopefully get a message to Master Mikao. I took my alone time to explore some of the castle, but there wasn't much to it. A bunch of extra rooms meant for guests.

When I stumbled upon the training yard, I found Alistair training with a wooden dummy. "Now that I don't have my shadows, I can't let my other skills get rusty."

"I hope someday you can forgive me," I said as I approached him.

"There is nothing to forgive. If I met the person responsible for killing my mate, I'd have done the same thing." He smiles, puts his blade down, and then waves me to a table. "I think we can do some training with The Devil card, right?"

I nod and sit across from him as he pulls it out and places it in the center.

"A few things to know about this one. It means false truths, but there

58

are several other subsidiary meanings to that as well. The one I intend for us to use it for would be to create a truth that the Amazon Queen will believe." I raise a brow, not understanding.

Alistair stands and walks over to the training armor, picking up a helmet to bring it back to the table. He sits again. "The Queen will look upon this helmet and believe it to be my head."

"I've seen someone use this card before. She used to disguise herself as another person. I initially believed it, but something about her gave it away." Odith was a vile person.

"That makes being a Tarot Master a gift and a curse. There is a temptation in this power, Serena. If you treat them right, they will protect you and provide for you, but if you abuse them, they will–"

"Turn against you." I interrupt, remembering what happened with Odith.

"So you do have some experience with them."

"You have no idea," I mumble, but he still hears me.

"Someday, if you want you can tell me, but for now, I want you to focus on your deck. You can't use mine, but imagine this card.

The first step is communicating with them. Once you accomplish that, then we can move on to step two." he states.

"And how many steps are in this process?"

"Just focus on this one." I do as I'm told, pulling my deck from my pocket and imagining The Devil card. When there's a magic zap between my fingers and the painted parchments, I pull the card but sigh when it's wrong. "You won't get it in one day. You have a couple of hours before you need to get ready. Use this time and keep trying. Once you accomplish this, tell me, and we will continue."

After Alistair leaves, I keep trying, and with each card I pull, it becomes apparent I'm not the only one with the cards. Hours pass, and my fingers become numb to their feel as my eyes grow weary. Just as I contemplate giving up, I draw one last card, only to be interrupted by Davi calling my name before I can examine it.

"It's time to get ready for your wedding." I stand and walk over to him. "Also, Braxor has arrived with Master Mikao and the dragon bones I need."

"Alwin's connection to him is strong," I admit.

"Practicing your pulls? What card did you get?" Davi looks at my hand, and I eye the card.

"The Devil."

"And that means?"

"Step one is done." I push past him and race to my chambers. Excitement fills me, as well as nerves.

I'm getting married and becoming a Queen all in one night. Mother would've never believed this.

ALWIN

I never thought I'd see the day of my wedding. Before Serena, the idea of finding my mate and wife hadn't crossed my mind. The priority was always ensuring the freedom of those born like me— half-bloods or, as the humans called us: half-breeds. The world I pictured had a half-blood sitting on the throne, banning any laws against us. In a perfect world, no unnecessary bloodshed or prejudices would exist.

With Serena by my side, that vision has become more apparent and vital than last night. Deciding to bring a child into this world was quickly the fastest 'yes' I could've given to my mate. Everything and anything she's ever desired is going to be delivered to her on a silver platter. I wouldn't be standing here dressed in a finely tailored black suit if that weren't the case.

My hair is combed and pulled back in a half-up fashion. There is no color on me, and that is alright with me. The boots I'm wearing have been shined bright enough. You can see my reflection staring back at me, and I was given a scented oil to wear. I chose not to because it smelled too much like spiced rum, and I didn't want my bride to think I needed to drink to survive this march down the aisle.

A knock sounded at my door, and Davi peeked his head inside. As our designated ring carrier, he was given a position of honor to stand at the altar with us. Alistair would be in with the crowd as it wasn't deemed appropriate for the former ruler to be seen with the new ones. The announcement of his stepping down so that his nephew and nephew's new bride would take over the reign of Silver City came as a shock to most of the citizens. As I stood by his side when we made the message from the balcony of the second level, I was anxious.

Would they revolt against us? Can I truly trust my uncle? So many thoughts were coursing through my brain that I didn't hear most of what he said until there was an uproar of cheers from the people below us.

"When my nephew found me, I was overjoyed by the news of his survival of the purge of our kind. I want you all to show your love and support for him as he takes my place as the new Shadow King of Silver City. His bride and fated is the Phoenix Queen we've all been waiting for." Alistair finished.

I scanned the crowd and saw a mix of admiration, intrigue, anger, and disappointment. It was unsettling.

"Say something." My uncle encouraged me.

I moved forward and, looking at no one in particular, began, "Thank you, Uncle. I first would like to commend you all on how fine a community you've helped build and maintain. I've never seen anything like this back where I'm from. Serena and I come to you willing to aid in whatever ailments you need resolving."

"We don't have any!" One person shouted.

"This city is a peaceful, thriving place. We don't want another King." Another protested, and others agreed, making the gathered crowd restless.

"Our intentions are not to rob you of your ruler. Alistair will remain at our side to advise and guide us in the ways of this wondrous city. There are threats outside of your barrier some of you don't know about. But I assure you, they are genuine." I swallowed as that made them go silent. Every eye on me, every ear hanging on each word passing my lips. "Those of you that are not of pure-blood, meaning coming from a sole lineage of a single species, there is a mighty Queen in the realm of Xora that would have you killed or go through convergence. Death is the likely result at her hand. It has been my mission for a century to rid this universe of genocide against our kind. I've lost many friends in this quest, but they've each taught me something before departing this world." I think of everyone that we lost during Odith's attack as it's the most recent.

"You have sanctuary here, which I don't intend to jeopardize. But I only ask for your help in return. Serena and I intend to fight this Queen's armies and overthrow her reign of terror, but for us to do so, we need an army. One that is willing and capable to fight against those that have essence. Whether it is the simplest form of controlling a single element or being a Tarot Master, all wielders are welcome to join us in this fight to free our brothers and sisters from certain death." Head turns, and whispers echo throughout. "Please do not feel obligated. But I ask that if you are volunteering, you come to the palace the day after my wedding and submit your name.

"There is great honor in serving a cause as noble as this. Freedom comes at a price, and some of you will pay it. The God of Death doesn't give life without intending to take it. Thank you for your continued support and loyalty during this haste transition."

"Alwin? Hello, oh fates, are you getting cold feet?" Davi's hand waving in my face has me blinking away the memory of this morning.

"No. Has Braxor arrived with Master Mikao?" That was another eventful hour. Calling on my friend used a lot of my strength, but when I finally reached him down our bond, the reception was clear. It turns out he's been in this realm before, and although he didn't like the sound of using dragon bones for a spell, he understood the need for it.

"Yes. They know to speak with you after tonight's proceedings." he answered.

"Okay. Let's get this thing started." I follow Davi to the throne hall, where both ceremonies will occur. One right after the other, and see it's packed with no one we know besides Master Mikao. Braxor, I imagine, is somewhere on the outside because he's much too large to fit inside this hall. The Master of Ceremonies is at the center, dressed in a white suit with golden floral imprints sewn into his sleeves. He looks about my uncle's age, only in human years.

"Welcome, Sire." He bows respectfully, and I grimace at the word.

"Thank you, but I'm not King yet," I whisper.

"True, but in an hour, you will be," I smirk at the older man, unsure how to respond. Alistair said this man had performed several weddings over the years and even knighthoods, guard hoods, and cruising of newborns.

Trumpets sounded, and the crowd rose as the announcement of my bride entering caught all of our attention. When the double doors opened, I couldn't believe my eyes. Serena was dressed in an off-the-shoulder gown of black and crimson feathers. All are sewn to perfection, representing the colors of our imprint, our essence. When she reached for my hand, I gladly took it, unable to concentrate on anything or anyone else but her.

"Beautiful." Is what I whispered, and I saw a pink color rise in her cheeks. Her hair was pinned to the top of her head to expose her face.

The words exchanged between us comprised traditional vows of devotion, duty, loyalty, and love—sentiments already deeply rooted between us. However, it was the sealing kiss that truly made it all feel real. Our lips meet in desire and passion. My wife and I didn't hold back, dipping her, skimming her body with my hands until I could lift her into my arms. Serena retained some semblance of control as she broke from my embrace.

"Alwin, we have an audience and still need to move on to the coronation."

"It's your fault, Firebird. If you wouldn't look so damn editable right now, I'd have control over my need to taste you. To fuck you on that throne again." She gasped, and I smiled but nodded my understanding. "To be continued."

The Master of Ceremonies gave us both a look of curiosity before gesturing to his helper to bring forth the two crowns and scepter. They laid on a velvet pillow of blue and looked heavier than I expected.

"With the power gifted to me by the fates and our former sovereign, Alistair, Shadow King of Silver City, I crown thee, Serena Ozark, Phoenix Queen, and her mate, Alwin, King of Shadows." Serena let out a heavy breath when her crown was placed upon her head, and as we took each other hand and hand, scepter in her other free, the crowd welcomed us with an uproar of cheers. When the ceremony ended, I carried my new wife to our chambers and discarded our clothing on the floor.

When I was on top of her, my lips meeting hers as she wrapped her legs around me, I could think of no better way to end this day than buried inside of her. I peppered her body with kisses until landing on her navel. A new life would soon blossom inside her womb, and I wanted our child to know me by voice.

"This is your father speaking." Serena giggled. "One day, you will be born, and things will be expected of you, but don't be afraid because you will have a wonderful mother to help you navigate this chaotic universe."

"Alwin, we don't know if I will immediately become a child. It could take months."

I smiled at her and moved back up her body, looking deep into her eyes as I said, "Then I guess we better keep practicing."

Our night was long, but I wouldn't change it for anything. After spilling my seed in her on the bed, we moved to the bath, then against the wall, and finally finished with her bent over the balcony looking out at our new home. We fell asleep that night in pure bliss, thoughts of war and destruction completely abolished from our minds as we looked forward to our family's future.

* * *

"Alwin and Serena must stay here while they continue to train.

It's the only way to ensure the victory of this upcoming war." Alistair starts our meeting of council members.

Braxor is on the edge of the courtyard, which we decided was the best place to have this meeting. Davi is close to finishing the restoration spell, which means that Serena needs to fine-tune her power over The Devil card for our deception to work.

"I agree. Alwin has much to learn if he intends to become a healer. Although powerful, Serena still needs to trust in herself when mastering the cards." Master Mikao adds.

"Why are you two talking as if we're not sitting across from you?" she asks. "I pulled The Devil card yesterday and have many times over today. I'm ready for the next step."

"We'll see about that. Turning one object into another requires a lot of essence and concentration." Alistair argues. "If we send that boy into the lion's den with a faulty illusion, he'll be killed, and your friends will never be freed."

"First off, I'm a grown man; secondly, Serena, as much as I admire you, and believe me, I do, I am powerless against the Amazon Queen, and I don't want to walk in there thinking I have his head in my bag when it's just a rusty old soldier's helmet." Davi inputs.

"Fine. Give me another day to learn this new skill. I don't want to waste any more time debating on when to act when Niya and Rose have been with those druids for almost two months. Please, Alistair, I must try at least to summon the illusion. I want it to be ready by the time Davi's Runes are finished being restored." Serena pleads.

I look towards Braxor, who is unusually quiet.

"Will your dragon armies be ready for when we need them?" I ask him.

"Don't worry about my colonies, Dark One. If we're needed, we'll be there." Braxor garbles.

"Then it's settled. The Queen and King will stay here to master their skills while the Rune Master sets forth to free the Confessor and Pixie. The war strategy will begin once we're all safe within Silver City's confides." Alistair finishes.

With the meeting finished, Davi races off to the Apothocary chambers, and Serena follows Alistair to begin training again. Braxor bids me farewell until my need for him to return is called upon, leaving me and Master Mikao in the courtyard. He's silent, and I know it's because he is finding words of wisdom to reassure me that everything that has happened up to this point was always meant to happen.

"Your mate is with child, Dark One. Sending her into battle may not be wise."

"How do you know?" I ask.

"My connection to the spiritual world is strong. That's an advantage and blessing when one becomes a Reiki Master. There's a soul already blooming inside of her."

"It's been a day, maybe two, since we, you know." I don't wish to talk about fucking my wife with one of the most respected men of my time.

He chuckles. "Being a celebrity does not deprive me of the knowledge one becomes with a child. But although the seedling is just that, you will feel the child's soul in time just as easily as I do."

"I see. Is that the first lesson in my apprenticeship?"

"As much as I would like to take you on as my apprentice, Alwin, there are things that you need to do to earn that honor. I can't simply give it to you because we're old friends. As much as I value our relationship, it would be a disservice to you and those around us to take you under my figurative wing without testing your intentions."

"My intentions are honorable."

"That is what you say, but to know one's heart and soul is different than knowing one's mind, as the three can be at war with one another." Master Mikao approaches me, placing a gentle hand over the beating organ. "You have great darkness inside of you, Shadow King, but being that your mate is full of light, that can balance it out. I know you know this, but Reike has powers beyond healing. Like all magic, it can be manipulated and used for darker deeds."

"What does that mean? I've never heard of Reiki being used for nefarious means."

He sighs. "That's because each master has done their best to prevent such occurrences from happening. But it didn't erase the past."

"You mean someone has used it for evil?" Master Mikao separates himself from me, stepping back before pulling out a chair to sit.

"There was an incident many centuries ago where a young pupil discovered necromancy. Which is the opposite of what Reike is. Your uncle has pulled you back, but it was a matter of minutes. That's the fine line between the two powers. Necromancy is used after days of death, but Reike can be used within minutes. If you combine the teachings of the two, the result is catastrophic." I take my seat from him, showing him I'm ready to listen and learn. No matter what he says, I will do whatever it takes if I need to prove myself to him. "I'm hesitant to teach you, Alwin, because of the shadows inside of you. Your power is one of the closest things to death there can be, aside from the darker arts. Reiki is about light and healing. I would be more inclined to teach Serena."

"But she's already getting her feet wet with the cards; adding this one might be too much," I state. "What must I do to prove I am the right pick? That I can use my essence for good."

Master Mikao lowers his momentarily and meets my eye before saying, "You must purge the shadows from your soul. Then and only then will I be willing to teach you."

Epilogue

A Rose will rise, a Raven will cry, and the skies will bleed when the Rune Master dies.

In this next chapter, the Rune Master Davi must take the hard- headed pixie Rose to the Realm of Masters so she can take on her destiny as the next Rune Master. Meanwhile, in the clutches of the Amazon Queen, Niya's situation grows more dangerous as she tries to free herself and her Griffon. With the growing power inside of her, leaving the ship proves more difficult than she was prepared for.

What will happen when these three unlikely friends meet fate end? What do the cards store for our young Confessor and her mate? Will Davi do the right thing and hand over his title and power to the one the Runes have chosen?

About the Author

About The Author

C.M. Hano is a talented writer and a dedicated mother of three wonderful children. Her love for Disney, magic, and princesses is reflected in her writing, full of romance and adventure. She is an expert at weaving magical tales that transport readers to enchanting realms of wonder and excitement. In many of her stories, dragons play a central role, which is no surprise, given that they are her favorite magical creatures. C. M. Hano's writing is a delightful blend of imagination, creativity, and heart, and her stories will surely captivate anyone who loves a good fairy tale.

Stay In Touch
Facebook: C. M. Hano
TikTok: @cmhanoauthor
Twitter(X): HanoCera
Instagram: @cerahano
Facebook Reading Group: C. M. Hano's Reading Warriors

You can connect with me on:

- 🌐 https://linktr.ee/cmhanoauthor
- 🐦 https://x.com/hanocera
- 📘 https://www.facebook.com/cmhano
- 🔗 https://www.tiktok.com/@cmhanoauthor
- 🔗 https://www.instagram.com/cerahano